TRY A BITE, TRILOBITE!

BY JONATHAN FENSKE

Ready-to-Read

Simon Spotlight

New York   London   Toronto   Sydney   New Delhi

For Walker, who REALLY LIKES noodles —J. F.

SIMON SPOTLIGHT
An imprint of Simon & Schuster Children's Publishing Division
1230 Avenue of the Americas, New York, New York 10020
This Simon Spotlight edition August 2023
Text and illustrations copyright © 2023 by Jonathan Fenske
All rights reserved, including the right of reproduction in whole
or in part in any form.
SIMON SPOTLIGHT, READY-TO-READ, and colophon are registered
trademarks of Simon & Schuster, Inc.
For information about special discounts for bulk purchases, please contact
Simon & Schuster Special Sales at 1-866-506-1949
or business@simonandschuster.com.
Manufactured in the United States of America 0723 LAK
2 4 6 8 10 9 7 5 3 1
Library of Congress Cataloging-in-Publication Data
Names: Fenske, Jonathan, author, illustrator.
Title: Try a bite, trilobite / by Jonathan Fenske.
Description: Simon Spotlight edition. | New York : Simon Spotlight, 2023.
Series: Ready-to-read: Level 1 | Audience: Ages 4 to 6.
Summary: Picky Trilobite only likes to eat noodles,
but when he tries a bite of Bug's snack, he is pleasantly surprised.
Identifiers: LCCN 2022051558 (print) | LCCN 2022051559 (ebook) | ISBN 9781665932660
(hardcover) | ISBN 9781665932653 (paperback) | ISBN 9781665932677 (ebook)
Subjects: CYAC: Food habits—Fiction. | Insects—Fiction. | LCGFT: Animal fiction. | Picture books.
Classification: LCC PZ7.F34843 Tr 2023 (print) | LCC PZ7.F34843 (ebook) |
DDC [E]—dc23
LC record available at https://lccn.loc.gov/2022051558
LC ebook record available at https://lccn.loc.gov/2022051559

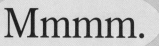

Mmmm.

Yum.

Wow.

Chew.

Chew.

Chew.

Gulp.

What do you think?

Hmmm.

I think I should try another bite.

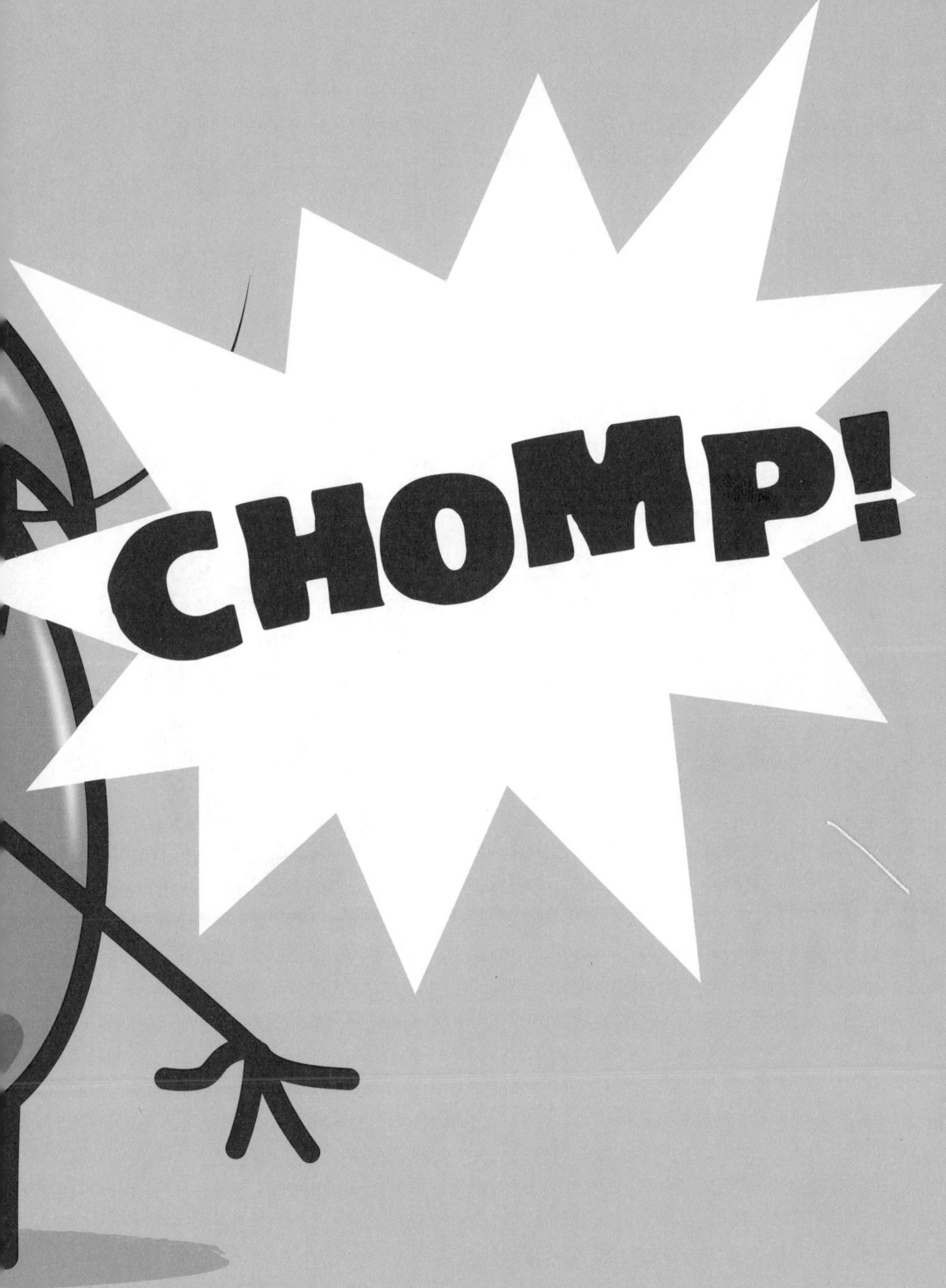
CHOMP!